How Hope Became an Activist

by George M. Johnson
&
illustrated by Danielle Grandi

*To Charlotte,
Hope you like
Hope's story!
Best wishes,
George Johnson*

How Hope Became an Activist
written by George M. Johnson
illustrated by Danielle Grandi

Copyright © 2020 Dixi Books
All rights reserved. No part of this book may be reproduced or transmitted to any form or by any means, electronic or mechanical, including photocopying, recording, or by any information and retrieval system, without written permission from the publisher.
First published in September 2020
ISBN: 978-1-913680-00-8

Dixi Books
20-22 Wenlock Road, London
England, N1 7GU

www.dixibooks.com
info@dixibooks.com

© Fairtrade Canada

This Mark appears on products which have been independently audited and adhere to international standards of Fairtrade.

How Hope Became an Activist

by George M. Johnson
&
illustrated by Danielle Grandi

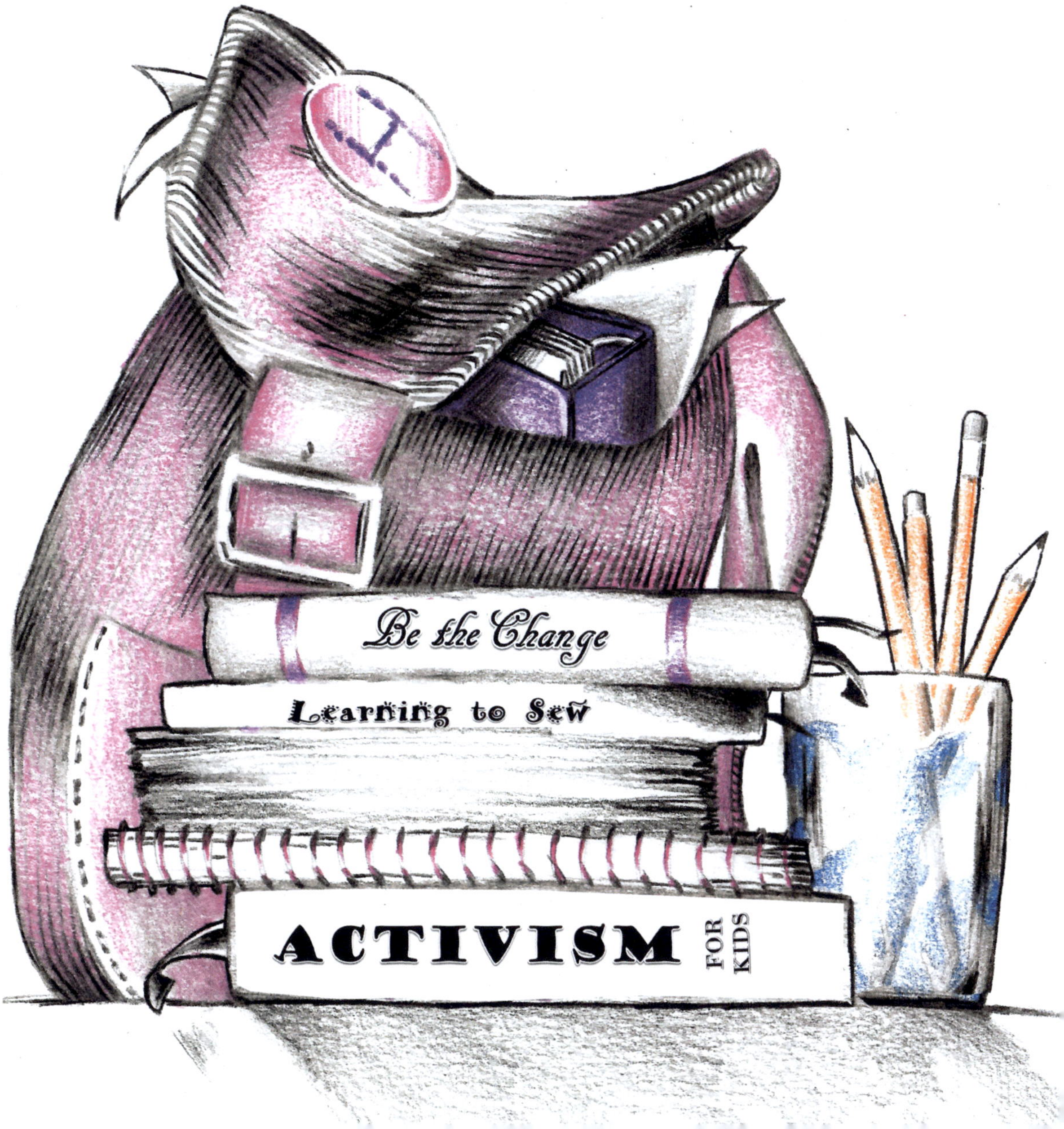

At first, I didn't even know what an activist was.

One day, when I was hanging around in my favourite tree, Mum came out and said, "Hope, how would you like to be in a play, an activist play?"

"Well, I love to play, and I'm pretty active." I swung down onto the ground – with a thump.

"I don't know how you do that." Mum smiled. "What I mean is, perform in a play. By activist, I mean an action that makes people aware of a need for change on an issue."

"Being in a play could be fun, I guess." My toes curled. "What issue?"

"Sweatshop labour in the clothing industry."

"Oh."

"Check your t-shirt label."

I twisted like a pretzel to see the back of my shirt. "It says, Made in Honduras. Where's that?"

"A country in Central America."

"Why was it made there?"

"Companies can get girls to make clothes cheaply, so cheaply that the girls cannot live well, or even eat properly."

"No way."

Mum nodded and frowned. "Some girls are as young as you. They work such long hours to support their families that they can't go to school."

I crossed my arms and said, "I'll do it."

At the first rehearsal, the Director asked me to play a girl sewing at an old, beat-up machine.

I scrunched my nose.

"Don't worry," she said, "You don't have to sew. You just have to look exhausted."

"I can do that. I like to stay up late, and Mum says I look exhausted all the time."

The Director laughed.

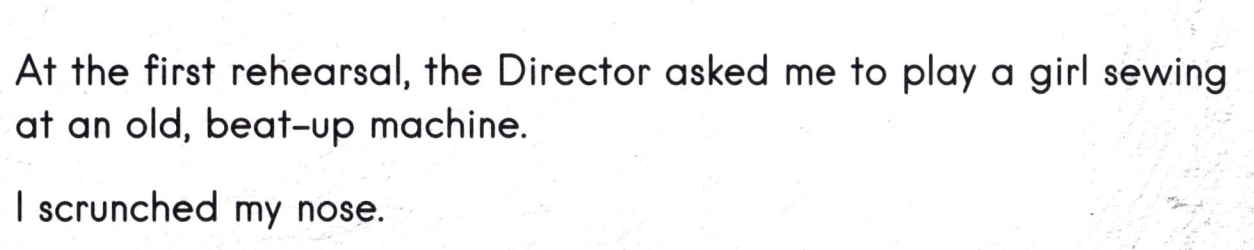

Once the play called "Martha's Donning of A"wear"ness" got going, there were some scary bits.

The factory boss named Brutus was shouting at the girls. I slid down my chair.

He wouldn't even let us go to the toilet, that is, in the play.

I wanted to shout 'That's not fair,' but I couldn't.

I was glad to go to school the next day. When I told my friends Parveen, Soo, and Jenny about the play, they wanted to join in.

The Director said, "Sure. There's strength in numbers."

Our first performance was at the Farmer's Market. My knees shook, and I was sweating, but that was good because I think the girls in Honduras must be nervous too.

People clapped loudly afterwards. A man rushed up to me and said, "Wow, I had no idea children were being treated like that to make clothes."

"I felt sad," I said, "sitting there, not being able to talk, with all the machine noise. It must be so hard for those girls."

The man nodded and a tear slid down his cheek. "Do you know which labels we should avoid?"

"I'm not sure. Some clothes are made in places with poor working conditions like Bangladesh, Cambodia, and Myanmar, and then have buttons added in our country so that the label says they are made here instead. You could look for the FAIRTRADE Mark.

It means that the workers have been treated fairly and received a fair price for their work."

Talking this over with my friends, I got an idea.

"What if we held a fashion show to help people understand the stories behind the clothes they wear?"

"Yeah, that sounds good," said Jenny.

"But how would we find out?" asked Parveen.

"We could do some research," I said, "and our parents might help."

Before long, we were working on our anti-fashion show, called "Are Your Clothes Really Clean?" Our new friend Sean got some bigger kids to help model.

Afterwards, we were pretty excited when people asked us where to get clothes made fairly. We decided to buy locally made and gently used clothes, or to check for the FAIRTRADE Mark if we buy clothes from other countries.

When the show closed, my new friend Vivian said, "Hey, you know I joined this group called Refugees and Friends Together, or RAFT."

"RAFT. That's a cool name," said Soo.

"It makes me think of a life raft," I said.

"Exactly," said Vivian. "The group is helping a family to come from Syria, to save their lives."

"Really? Why do they want to come here?" asked Jenny.

"They will be safe here," said Vivian, "but they won't have anything. They need people to collect stuff for them, and to help their children learn English. Could you help?"

"Sure," I said, along with the others, and we all hugged.

Mum came up to me and said, "I'm so proud of you. Now, I guess you know what it means to be an activist."

"You mean, getting everybody active to do something good?"

"That's right."

"I know we are small but it feels like we are creating something bigger than us. Our actions might help kids we don't even know. Plus, I've made friends being an activist."

"You have, and now you're part of a community of people with positive energy. One activist, Martin Luther King Jr., said that injustice anywhere is a threat to justice everywhere because we are all woven together like a single piece of clothing."

I thought of those girls in Honduras, who needed food and a safe home and wanted to go to school, just like me. "I guess we are all connected."

My heart felt big in my chest and a tingle ran through me.

Then I knew, a better world is possible – if we work on being activists and make good changes happen.